# ABC's for the Little Trinis (In All of Us)

Andrea Hall

# DEDICATION

**For Cruz**

# CONTENTS

# ACKNOWLEDGMENTS

*"A people's art is the genesis of their freedom"- Claudia Jones*

Looking back at my early journal entries in 2011, I had the desire to curate an encyclopedia of Trinbagonian culture to help instill a sense of pride in my future children. Honestly, I wrote this goal after attending a J'ouvert event. I overheard a young man saying he was excited about it but didn't really know what it meant. There are so many generations of Trinbagonians globally that may not know the origins of our cultural practices, our stories, and our rich history.

Growing up, I'd hear stories from my grandmothers and my parents about Trinidad's folklore characters and our extraordinary leaders. One of my uncles claimed to have seen a La Diablesse in Santa Cruz. My father, who doesn't really "believe in dem tings," had his own experience of being followed by an entity dressed in white on the Old Main Road. Hearing stories that would raise the hairs on your arms were a staple of my childhood.

My intention with this project is to keep our history and heritage alive. In this first collection, *ABC's for the Little Trinis* introduces folklore and culture in a simple and digestible format. Some of these characters are unique to Trinbago, while others are known across the diaspora. When I began researching these topics, it was unsurprising that a lot of our history is written from a colonial Eurocentric perspective. There's a saying that "the clues to our history has been left by the ancestors around us." Our folklore, detailing magic and morality, influences learned behaviors and forms a complicated and rich tapestry of our past. You can ask elders how to get rid of a soucouyant and you might get varied responses. I hope that this project serves as a conversation starter to connect the older and younger generations. Our art, rooted in resistance, is the outlet to our freedom.

This book is for everyone, from those that are closely connected to their heritage to those removed from their roots and wanting to reconnect. It's for the kids like me who had to quickly lose their accent and code-switch when moving to "foreign," it's for the "Trini to de bone" living in Trinbago or abroad, it's for the people who come to visit and fall in love with the culture. Let these characters inspire you to connect with the culture and keep strong ties to your family's generational stories. As much as our culture is commoditized, don't lose sight of the history.

So, Mami and Kevin, thanks for being a sounding board. Cruz, even though you're not here yet, you are my biggest inspiration for completing this project. To my family in Santa Cruz and in the States. Love you all.

# ANANSI [AH-nan-see]

Anansi is an admired folklore character throughout the diaspora. Originating in the Akan tribe in West Africa, it's believed that Anansi stories made their way to the Caribbean during the slave trade. Anansi is often depicted as a spider but can also take human form. There are various Anansi stories meant to teach you a moral lesson, and some remind us of how cunning and crafty he can be. Anansi can outwit creatures that are bigger and bolder than him for his personal gain. Back in the day, these stories were inspirational and entertaining. During enslavement and post-emancipation, people connected to them because Anansi displayed resilience during harsh conditions. Families often gathered around at night and shared these stories with their children and grandchildren. In true folklore storytelling fashion, don't forget to end with, "Crick crack, monkey break he back for a piece of pomerac. Wire bend, and so the story end." Some people say that you should always end all folklore stories with this phrase to prevent jumbies from following you.

# BUCK [buhk]

The buck is short in stature with sharp teeth, long arms, and long claws. Though menacing in appearance, this little creature will grant whatever you wish – conditionally, of course. It's said that affluent families journeyed through the jungles of Guyana to bring the buck to Trinidad. People who have a buck become successful or get rich too quick. There have always been rumors that some eminent business owners have a buck and often have to make sacrifices to keep their buck happy. Traditionally, I've heard that to keep a buck happy, you must feed it with milk and bananas. But sometimes milk and bananas aren't enough, and the price to pay is a human soul. If you fail to feed your buck, don't follow its directions, or neglect it in any way, you'll end up paying with a life. To get rid of a buck, you have to catch it, put in a bottle, and then throw it into an ocean or river. So, you might want to reconsider opening a random bottle that you find washed ashore.

# COLIBRI LEGEND [co-lee-bree]

The Pitch Lake is widely known as the 8th Wonder of the World. But few know how the lake came to be. Thousands of years ago, the Chima tribe who lived in the exact location of the lake, celebrated a massive victory over a neighboring tribe. They wore colibri (hummingbird) feathers and had a decadent feast devouring the sacred birds. Overcome with excitement, they forgot that hummingbirds are the spirit of their ancestors. The gods sought to punish them for their actions. Pimlonta, the winged god, opened up the earth which swallowed the tribe. Makonaima, the Creator, then commanded Pimlonta to fill the earth with pitch so that the Chima people can never escape.

# DOUEN [du-en]

There's a saying that you should never shout a child's name out loud because they could end up gone forever. Why? Because of the douens. Douens are spirits of children who weren't baptized. They are the only entity in our folklore that can straddle the realms of good and evil. A douen will listen to a parent call a child's name and imitate it. Children innocently thinking it's a friend or a relative calling them often end up lost in the woods, never to be found again. These little faceless souls lurk in the forest and near your homes with wide brim hats and feet turned backward. They really just want someone to play with them. If you hear someone calling your name and the sweet sound of laughter, don't follow the living dead.

# EBENEZER "PAPA NEEZER" ELLIOTT

Papa Neezer was Trinidad's renowned healer, or "obeah man." Legend has it that he gained his powers at the age of 32 while napping in his garden. He dreamed that he could cast out demons and had the power to heal. While napping, a snake crawled over him, and it left him unharmed. He took this as a sign that he was bestowed with spiritual powers. Papa Neezer was a descendant of the Merikens, a group of free African-Americans that arrived in Trinidad around 1815. Merikens were enslaved runaways who fought for the British in the War of 1812. For their service, the British granted these soldiers their freedom and land in South Trinidad.

He grew up as a London Baptist and became intrigued with Orisha practices. It's believed that he practiced both faiths until he died. In Trinidad, the perception of him is that he was a powerful obeah man. Even the calypsonian Mighty Sparrow mentioned him in the song "Obeah Wedding," singing that someone else's obeah can't upset his plans because his grandfather is the great Papa Neezer. Despite his notoriety, during those days, many people generalized any practice that was not Christianity as "obeah." They held the belief that ancestral religious practices are "bad." The people that knew him well described him as a thoughtful healer. He was known to cure the sick, get rid of maljo (evil eye), and drive away evil spirits.

# FAIRYMAID

In Tobago, stories about fairymaids and mermen are known across generations. Fairymaids are beautiful, with smooth skin, lush thick hair, piercing eyes, and a tiny deer hoof. They will lure mortal men and wipe them of their senses. Mermen who dwell in the deep-sea north of the island come to the river caves to mate with fairymaids.

Fairymaids are known to bestow gifts to mortal men. They'll take a man under the water for 15 days, and when he surfaces, he'll be rewarded with beauty, increased fortune, or skills. They're also known to take a man's shadow, which will make him demented. To get his shadow back, he must go to the river, plead for it, leave the water, and not look back. If a man wants to end a relationship with a fairymaid, he must offer two pairs of shoes. He has to burn the first pair. The fairymaid will rise out of the water and ask, "Should I be paid for past services?" He should then respond, "Nothing but this pair of shoes" and throw the second pair in the water. If a fairymaid ever chases you down a lonely road, turn a corner. Despite their many gifts, legend has it that turning corners is something they can't do. Back in the early 20th century, a doctor was chased by a fairymaid and he was only able to escape by turning a corner on the road. Fairymaid and mermen stories are endless. Just ask around and you'll hear some unbelievable tales.

# GANG GANG SARA
# THE WITCH OF GOLDEN LANE

Sara was a witch that was "blown away" from her home in Africa and wound up on the Golden Lane plantation in Les Coteaux, Tobago. She married Tom, an enslaved man who she knew back in her village when she was a child. In Les Coteaux, she was known for her kindness and the wisdom she imparted. After Tom died, she wanted to return to her village in Africa. She climbed the silk cotton tree and took flight. Tragically, Sara plummeted to the ground and died. Sara was not aware that she broke one of the primary rules of witchcraft; she ate food with salt which stripped her of her powers to fly. Sara was buried next to Tom in the plantation cemetery, which still exists today. Their tombstones are among the few for the enslaved people who lived on the Golden Lane plantation.

# HYARIMA [HI-ah-ree-ma]

Hyarima, a Nepuyo chief, lives on as one of Trinidad's most prolific freedom fighters. In 1625 he escaped from enslavement under the Spanish encomienda system and fled to the hills of Arima. He was a guerrilla fighter, leading resistance movements against the Spanish. It's said that he was one of the key figures that influenced the Arena massacre.

On December 1st, 1699, Amerindians revolted against the Spanish. In the encomienda system, Amerindian people were beaten and tortured for refusing to assimilate. There are two theories on how this revolt transpired. One version of events states that the rebels ambushed priests that were on their way to visit a mission. In the alternate version, the rebels led an orchestrated plot agreeing to convert to Catholicism. They dressed up in colonial religious clothes and used this guise to launch their attack.

They killed the Spanish governor, the priests, and destroyed the church. Only one person in the governor's party managed to escape and ring the bell, sounding an alarm. The rebels threw the governor's body in the river and fled for the coast. Many chose death, jumping off the cliffs into the sea instead of getting captured by the Spanish.

Sadly, Amerindians continued to endure inhumane brutality at the hands of the Spanish after this revolt. Hyarima and his resistant movements are still remembered today. Hyarima devoted his life to protecting his people from colonizers who were determined to eradicate the Indigenous way of life.

# INDIAN MAS

There are many prominent Indian mas characters in Carnival that honor our nation's Indigenous peoples. The portrayals of some characters are a dying tradition. This is one of the main reasons why it's important to not only observe but to "play mas" to keep the tradition going.

**Black Indian:** Today there are very few Black Indian bands. The Black Indian mas portrayal honors the union of culturally mixed Amerindians and Africans in Trinidad. Part of the costume, the pants and blouse, mock the Spanish conquistadors. The rest pays homage to African and Indigenous influences. Faces are painted black, and the costume is adorned with corbeaux (vulture) feathers; a sacred bird for Black Indians. Black Indians are one of the few Carnival characters that have their own speech. Their language consists of words from Amerindian, African, French, and Spanish languages. When different Black Indian bands met in the street traditionally, they would face off, questioning each other to test their "realness." If you were a true Black Indian, you'd be able to answer.

**Blue Indian:** Blue Indians are similar to Warahoons. It's believed that the portrayal is based on a tribe originating in the Orinoco Delta. Blue Indians wear elaborate costuming and headpieces.

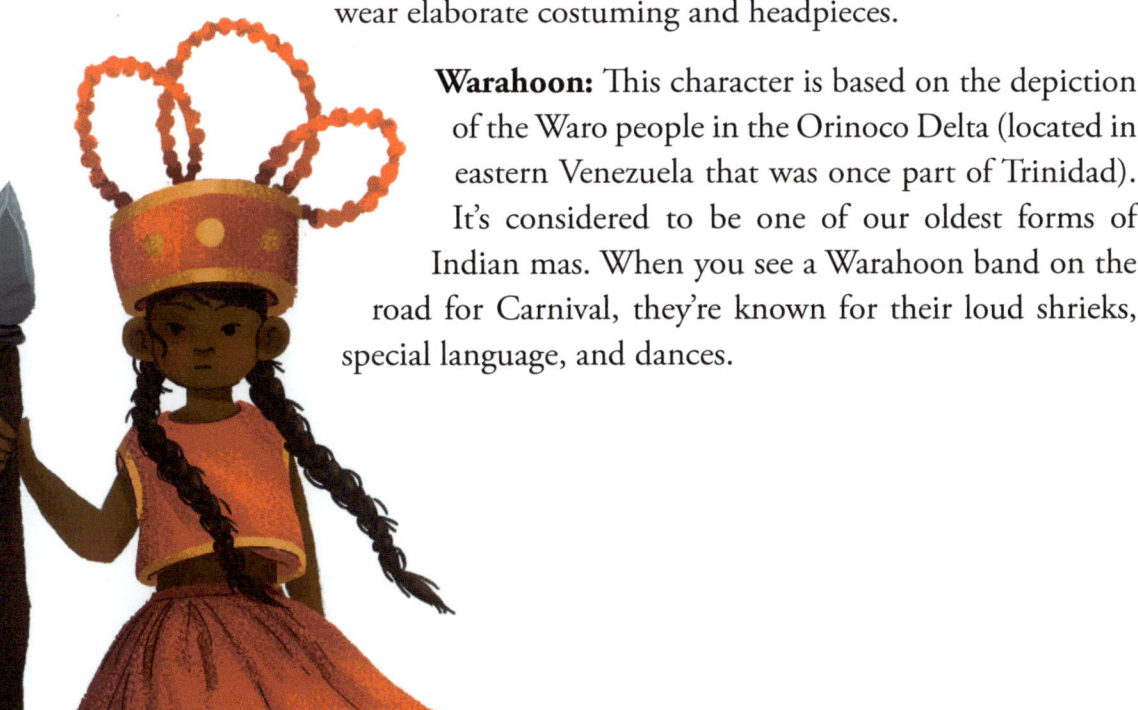

**Warahoon:** This character is based on the depiction of the Waro people in the Orinoco Delta (located in eastern Venezuela that was once part of Trinidad). It's considered to be one of our oldest forms of Indian mas. When you see a Warahoon band on the road for Carnival, they're known for their loud shrieks, special language, and dances.

# JUMBIE (MOKO) [MOH-ko]

Jumbies are typically troublesome and mischievous spirits in our culture. However, the Moko Jumbie is a protecting spirit. With roots in Africa, the Moko is believed to be a deity of retribution. He's known as the protector of the village. Towering over 10 feet high, he can see and sense evil faster than a mortal man. People often say that you can feel when Moko is near because the air smells sweet. This character stands elevated on 10-15 feet painted stilts and usually wears colorful pants or a skirt to cover them. In the early days of Carnival, Moko Jumbies danced through the streets of Port of Spain and collected money from people sitting in balconies and second-floor windows. You'll often see Moko Jumbies during Carnival and other cultural celebrations.

# KALINDA [KAH-lyn-da]

Kalinda is Trinbago's martial arts practice rooted in resistance. It's said that the style of Trinidad's stick fighting today was originated by Joe Talmana. His name is echoed in lavways (songs) across generations. Stick fighting originates in Central Africa, where warriors fought with a spiritually prepared stick (bois) four feet in length. In a stick fighting match, drummers provide the soundtrack, while the chantuelle (griot) engages the crowd with a call and response to energize the fighters. Seasoned fighters are calculated in their approach. Each step is deliberate; to some it may look like opponents are dancing before they strike their blows.

Post-emancipation, stick fighting became a major attraction during the canboulay ("cane burning") processions. Canboulay was a celebration to commemorate the end of enslavement. During slavery, when sugar fields caught on fire, enslaved people were rounded up and forced to collect cane, putting their lives in danger. The formerly enslaved reclaimed this act. Canboulay celebrations consisted of burning sugar cane, drumming, dancing, and songs that satirized plantation owners. In the dead of the night, revelers carried flambeaux through the wooden city. The plantation owners saw this as a threat to their existence. To partake in canboulay was an act of resistance.

Colonial powers sought to further oppress Black forms of expressions, and crush the "jamette carnival" (a French pejorative term for the working class residing in the barracks of Port of Spain and people who participated in Carnival). First, they banned masquerading, music, and dancing. In 1880, they outlawed all African percussion instruments. Yet, the bands grew larger with increased participants after attempts to shut down canboulay failed.

On February 28th, 1881, Chief Police Officer Captain Baker led 150 police officers to Market Street in Port of Spain to stop the canboulay celebrations. In a bloody clash, Joe Talmana dismounted Captain Baker from his horse and disappeared down the Spanish Main Road. This clash lasted three hours, leaving some dead and injured on both sides. This was a fight to honor their traditions. The governor later declared, "there shall be no interference with your masquerade."

Joe Talmana's name is echoed in lavways and soca songs today. Today stick fighting competitions pay tribute to the resistance and bravery of the ancestors. For a true "bois man" stick fighting is more than just "buss head" and bragging rights. It's about discipline; abstaining from meat, alcohol, and focusing on energy work to prepare. To win in a stick fighting match, you must be unyielding, graceful, and you must dance beautifully.

# LA DIABLESSE [LAH-jah-bless]

The La Diablesse, commonly known as the temptress or devil woman, is one of our most notable folklore characters.

My uncle claimed to have seen a La Diablesse. In Santa Cruz, right before you make your way into Cantaro Village, he spotted her under the full moon. She's beautiful as ever, with piercing eyes, brown skin, flowing hair, and a wide-brimmed hat (she's also been seen wearing a headwrap). She waits with her right foot planted on the road, and her cow hoof hidden in the grass. When men notice the cow hoof, it's often too late for them. As alluring as she is, she's twice as dangerous.

Old folk stories tell you she's so spellbinding, she will lead men into the forest, make them go mad, or even lead them off a cliff. Others claim men will follow her down the road, but they're never able to catch up to her. When he realizes this, he no longer has a shadow. In some cases, this means death or being driven to insanity.

My grandmother always tells a story about her friend Mr. Teddy, a taxi driver, who had an encounter with a La Diablesse. Late one night, he picked up passengers along his usual route, which included a beautiful woman. He dropped everyone off, and she was the last passenger remaining. Lighting his cigarette, he asked her, "Mam, where yuh want to stop?" At the same time, he heard a loud cackle and she disappeared. Needless to say, that was the last time he ever drove a taxi after sundown.

I've also heard she befriends men or sometimes stalks them down lonely roads. The old-timers say that if you encounter a La Diablesse, take off your clothes, turn them inside out, and put them back on again. This should protect you from her.

As beguiling as she is, the La Diablesse is the woman's revenge. It's believed that this character evolved from the goddess of love, Erzulie, and grew into a character of retribution. The La Diablesse preys on men who have wronged women in their life. So, if you're a "good guy" don't fear, she probably won't visit you.

# MAMA GLO

As early as the 18th and 19th centuries, the Kalinago people (Caribs) who lived in Arima and Valencia shared sightings of a beautiful woman with a snake body on the Valencia River. Oral stories passed down through generations also share encounters with this woman in the Matura Basins, to the extent that it's been named the Matura Mermaid Pools.

Farmers to fishermen often heard loud cracking sounds. This was her ophidian body crashing against the surface of the river. Mama Glo or "mother water," is the protector of the rivers, waterfalls, and the forest. People often saw her sitting on a rock or bathing in the river basin. According to older folktales, it is believed that she is Papa Bois' lover, as hunters sometimes spotted them together. If you anger her by overfishing, polluting the waters, harming the river animals, or desecrating the area in any way, you'll feel her wrath. When angered, she changes form with each strand of hair morphing into a snake. If she feels slighted, she'll submerge you and take you down to her water kingdom for hours. Sometimes the bodies never surface; not even the strongest swimmer can survive her attack. Old folks say that if you meet her in the forest and want to escape, take off your left shoe, turn it upside down, and quickly walk backward until you get home.

# NATIVES:
# THE ORIGINAL INDIGENOUS PEOPLES

Trinidad's Indigenous tribes ruled the land six thousand years before Spaniards washed up ashore. The Spanish conquistadors created gross generalizations about the Kalinago and Lokono tribes (commonly referred to as Caribs and Arawaks), which are still referenced in our history books and taught in schools. Because of colonization, and their depleted population, many of the original cultural practices remain unknown. However, Indigenous languages are embedded in our culture and, some folklore stories have survived for generations.

**Kalinago (Caribs):** The Kalinago were known to be "warlike" and "savage cannibals" because they allegedly burned their enemies' fat. But archaeologists do not have con-

*Kalinago (Caribs)*

crete proof of this. Kalinagos didn't welcome the Spanish invaders or trade with them, so one can only assume this is why these generalizations were made. They were described as stronger than the Lokonos because of their slightly taller stature. The Kalinago wore body paint for war and other celebratory moments; the women often painted themselves with roucou (red dye from a fruit). They believed in the evil spirit Maybouya; highly respected healers in their community had to pacify this entity through various rituals. Healers went through special training instead of following the standard path to becoming a warrior. Kalinago songs (carietos) were powerful; they were used to heal the sick, and strengthen men during battle, which resulted in many victories against the Spanish. One folktale recalls that Spanish soldiers ambushed two of the greatest Kalinago singers pouring metal down their throats because their songs threatened a Spanish victory.

**Lokono (Arawaks):** According to the Spanish, Lokono people were more "peaceful" than Kalinagos. While historical accounts state that they traded with the Spanish, there are also accounts that they were neither docile nor pledged fealty to them. History often pits the two tribes as rivals however they shared many similarities. They both ambushed and launched coordinated counterattacks against the Spanish and shared related beliefs. They were animistic and believed that everything had a spirit that connects to the gods. Lokono tribes in different regions of the Caribbean each had their own mythology on how the gods created the earth.

Today, there are still Indigenous peoples across various groups that still reside in Trinidad. The Santa Rosa Carib Festival and First Peoples Day seeks to honor and pay tribute to our nation's original inhabitants and their descendants.

*Lokono (Arawaks)*

# OLE MAS

Before Carnival evolved into what we know it as today, key characters masqueraded down the street. Today, we affectionately call these traditional characters 'ole mas.' Each has a uniquely rich history that is rooted in resistance. The formerly enslaved took on these characters to satire behaviors of slave owners and to remember and honor their past.

**Blue Devils:** There are different types of "devil mas" in Trinidad. Jab molassie is credited as the original devil mas. In Jab molassie mas, the formerly enslaved would cover themselves in molasses during the Carnival celebration. It's believed that their intention was to mock and offend plantation owners, painting themselves even darker when people were punished for being Black. It was also a way to disguise themselves when they saw oppressive forces during Carnival. Carrying a pitchfork, and wearing a chain or rope around their waist, this is an apt portrayal for years of subjugation. Traditional jab molassie characters played mas for money. They scared onlookers; it's either you get dirt, mud, and oil on you or you have to pay up. Hence the song, "Pay De Devil."

Traditionally, the character was brown but later evolved into Blue devils. Legend states that in the hills of Paramin, the forefathers of this practice didn't have access to molasses, so they used Crown Blue soap. A key part of blue devil mas is the performance. Blue devils are wild; with bloody tongues (food dye) they command the streets. Beating on tin cans (in earlier days they used tamboo bamboo), they have their unique rhythm passed down through generations. With milk to coat their throats and stomach and flambeaux in hand, they spit fire in the air, making light out of the darkness their ancestors endured.

**Dame Lorraine:** This character is a satire on the French plantocracy, specifically the French slaveholder's wives. The portrayal mocks their behavior at masquerade balls and their physical appearance with exaggerated body parts. Originally both men and women were masked as Dame Lorraine, but today only women dress up as this character.

**Pierrot Grenade:** Known for his whip and his wit, the Pierrot Grenade is one of the few speaking Carnival characters. While he doesn't use the whip, his tongue does the lashing. The Pierrot loves to show his knowledge by giving extravagant speeches. This is by no means a regular speech. He sets up the speech by telling the crowd what word he will spell and does this by using rhymes, allegory, and social commentary. He weaves a complex story for each syllable, leaving spectators in awe.

29

# PAPA BOIS [PAH-PAH BWAH]

Papa Bois is the guardian of the forest. For hundreds of years in Trinidad, there have been stories from hunters who encountered a half-man, half-animal creature. He's known to shapeshift, sometimes appearing as a deer to lead hunters into the deep woods, and then he shows them his true self, scaring them off. As protector of the forest, he sounds a cowbell to alert animals that hunters are near. It's said that if you run into Papa Bois, be polite and greet him with, "Bonjour, vieux Papa." If he's in a pleasant mood and engages with you, don't look at his feet. Be good to the animals and don't overhunt because he'll make his presence known.

# QUEEN'S PARK SAVANNAH

Spanning over 200 acres, this iconic green space in the heart of Port of Spain is the epicenter of Trinidad's Carnival, affectionately known as the "Greatest Show on Earth." Throughout the years, the Savannah has always played a key role in Trinbagonian culture. In 1738 and through the 1800s, the Peschiers, a French-Swiss family, used the land as a sugar plantation. When the British seized Trinidad, Madame Peschier agreed to sell with the condition that her family retained a piece of land in the middle of the estate as their burial ground. This is why you'll see the cemetery there today. Many years after the sale, it grew to be a place for cultural recreation.

In 1919, the first Carnival competition was held at Queen's Park Savannah. The Victory Carnival commemorated the end of World War I as there were no official Carnival celebrations during that time. During the early 1900s, the celebrations remained divided. The "upper-class elite" remained in their country clubs and had costume balls on their estates, while everyone else celebrated in the streets of Port of Spain. The elite stepped out on Carnival Monday and Tuesday in decorated trucks, and waved down at the crowds.

Eventually, during the 1940s, post World War II, Carnival became more integrated as people across different socio-economic lines grew to occupy the same spaces. 1955 ushered in the Band of the Year competition and a new concept of "pretty mas." In this era, designers constructed intricate costumes, dialing up their creativity using feathers, fiberglass, wire, sequins, and plastic molding. These designers birthed the grandeur of the modern-day Carnival.

Today, the Queen's Park Savannah remains the hub for Carnival competitions including the steelband competition also known as Panorama, the Kings and Queens costume competition, and Dimanche Gras (Carnival Sunday), where calypsonians battle for the title of Calypso Monarch.

# "ROBBER"
# MIDNIGHT ROBBER

The Midnight Robber is one of Carnival's most beloved characters. The Robber's prime influence is the African griot. Over the years the costume has evolved. In the past, Robbers wore cowboy styled wild west rancher outfits. Today, he dons a satin shirt, layered pants, a long cape, and a wide-brimmed hat to add intrigue. Before he speaks, he blows his whistle to command attention. The Midnight Robber's speech is embellished and boastful. In so many words, he'll tell you that he comes from a long line of men in history who wreaks havoc on the world and explain why you should be scared of him. The purpose of "robber talk" is to strike fear in your heart and get payment. Like many traditional mas characters, after he gives his speech, he'll collect money from spectators.

# SOUCOUYANT [SOO-KOO-YAH]

She is known as one of Trinidad's infamous shapeshifters. She is an isolated village woman by day who turns into a ball of fire and haunts the night sky for human blood. One morning, she returned through the keyhole in her door and called to her skin sitting in the mortar, "Skin skin come to me." But something was off; her skin remained shriveled up. She screeched, "Skin skin ya nah know me?!" One of the villagers put salt in her mortar while she was out preying on her next meal, causing her to meet her demise. She was never able to change into her human skin again. Salt is one way to get rid of a soucouyant. To reveal if a soucouyant is in your midst, sprinkle rice around her house or on the village roads. She'll spend the entire night counting the grains until the sun rises.

So, if you wake up one morning and see black and blue bruises on your skin as my grandmother would say, "Soucouyant bite yuh, make sure yuh put salt around de house."

# TREE (SILK COTTON)

A beautiful but monstrous tree, standing 80 feet high and five feet wide, the silk cotton tree is known to put a sliver of fear in a man's heart. The brave, when walking past the tree might walk a little faster or avoid it altogether if they can. Some government officials even refuse to cut down these trees and would rather let nature take its course.

Your grandmother might tell you that the silk cotton tree "does have a lot of funny ting, jumbie business." That's because many believe that jumbies and supernatural beings dwell in those trees. The Indigenous peoples thought it was a passageway to another world. The descendants of the enslaved also had great respect for the tree and knew not to alter it. You'll often hear stories about unusual sightings at silk cotton trees. If you were to cut any part of the tree, grave misfortunes would follow. For instance, a Ministry of Works personnel tampered with the silk cotton tree where Gang Gang Sara flew from and later suffered from a stroke.

Some folklore stories will tell you that origin of the tree holding spirits starts with Le Bois and Bazil the devil. Le Bois, a villager from Sangre Grange, was so cunning that he locked the devil Bazil away in a room in the tree. Bazil created chaos in this little village on the outskirts of a coal mine in Grande. Le Bois was proud that he outsmarted Bazil. For seven years, the village had no deaths. Papa God sent a Messenger to trick Le Bois into releasing Bazil to avoid overcrowding at the coal mine and overpopulation in Trinidad. Le Bois and his friends were at a rum shop liming, and of course, Le Bois grew boastful that he deceived Bazil. The Messenger tricked Le Bois into showing him where he kept Bazil locked up on the tree's seventh floor. They climbed each floor and went to each room until they reached the last floor. When Le Bois entered the room, Bazil snatched him, and he was never heard from again. From then, the legend of the most feared silk cotton tree was born.

My favorite silk cotton tree tale is "the baby story." A man was riding his bike on Belmont Circular Road at night and saw a baby nestled under the tree. Wondering why the child was there, he picked it up to take it to the hospital. As he started pedaling away from the tree towards the hospital, the baby's weight grew heavier. It felt like he was carrying a grown man. Dripping in sweat, he hears a booming voice, "Put meh down where yuh find me!" Startled, he peddled back towards the tree and the child no longer felt heavy. He put the baby back under the tree and sped off, thinking to himself if that had really just happened.

This tree is integral to folklore and spiritual practices. Some may brush off the real-life events that surround these trees as coincidental, but even the skeptics know to keep their distance.

# URIAH BUZZ BUTLER

Uriah Buzz Butler was a man of the people. He was a true activist and enemy of the colonial police state. Unhappy with the blatant disrespect, racism, and poor working conditions at the Apex Oilfields, he led a strike demanding better conditions. Butler played a pivotal role in organizing the labor movement and was a catalyst in protests across the country in 1937. His disappearance during the summer of 1937 became an urban legend.

Legend has it that Butler possessed "magical powers." One afternoon, the police stopped a car that he was in, and it is rumored that Butler disappeared into thin air. Another story says that police attempted to arrest him during a strike at an oil field, and he disappeared in the crowd. Calypsonian Atilla the Hun immortalized his disappearance in the song "Where was Butler?" Whether he actually possessed magical powers, or his loyal supporters protected him from the colonial police is up for debate. The impact of these protests changed the conditions for the poor working class. He birthed the modern labor movement, creating safe and fair labor conditions for all.

# VOODOO AND OBEAH

There's a misconception that voodoo and obeah are interchangeable. While they're not the same, the main commonality is that enslaved people used both to resist. Unlike voodoo, obeah isn't centered around deities. It has since evolved to include elements of Orisha, Catholicism, and Hinduism. Obeah was an outlet for the enslaved to protect themselves from the torturous hands of overseers and a way to heal themselves using bush medicine. The enslaved and later freed peoples sought practitioners for medical and spiritual guidance. Obeah was the impetus for many enslaved rebellions across the Caribbean. During slavery, overseers feared practitioners. Overseers often woke up with deadly sores all over their bodies, suffered inexplicable bodily harm, or simply turned up dead. The practice threatened stability on the plantation. As a result, the colonial government created laws to criminalize the practice, and obeah has remained stigmatized for generations.

These laws are one of the reasons why it's not recognized as a religion. Unlike other Afro-Caribbean religions, obeah lacks liturgy. It's believed that practitioners are born with special powers revealed to them through visions or dreams during their late teens or early adulthood. Powers are believed to be passed generationally from an elder to a child. If you aren't born with these powers, you need to be indoctrinated. The core of the practice still remains a mystery to outsiders.

Stories of obeah men and women are rampant in our folklore and everyday life. Practitioners are responsible for a lot of superstitions. Growing up, my grandmother warned me to never pick up money on the ground, especially money in a crossroad, because, "Yuh never know who do they thing an drop it dey." Meaning that you never want to disrupt a ritual that is not meant for you; otherwise it can backfire and cause severe damage.

Trinidad's most famous obeah woman was the polarizing Mother Cornhusk of Moruga (Catherine Brizan). She dreamed that St. Anthony gave her powers to heal. People came from near and far to visit her Healing School for help. Using bush medicine, she whipped up concoctions from spells for protection, to potions to help with fertility. While revered as a gifted healer, some critics accused her of doing more harm than good. Whether you supported her not, Mother Cornhusk left her mark on the island.

# WOLFMAN OR LAGAHOO

The wolfman, locally known as the lagahoo (loup garou) is one of our notorious shapeshifters. He's known to appear with chains wrapped around his waist, sometimes dragging a coffin filled with bush rum. He can morph into any animal from a fat pig, to a cow, or wild mare.

By day, the lagahoo is a "science man" or obeah man. It's said that he's well versed in the teetalbay, a study of syncretic dark magic spanning Afro Caribbean, Hindu-Caribbean, and European cultures. Some people say you can spot a lagahoo because they are extremely tall and slender with "clear eyes." To kill a lagahoo, you must beat it with a stick anointed by holy water. While beating it, the lagahoo might change into another animal like a wild bull or a vicious dog, but eventually, it'll disappear into the mist.

If you want to see a lagahoo, and not be seen by it, take yampee (mucus) from the corner of a dog's eye and put it in your eye. Then peep out of a keyhole at midnight.

# XYLOPAN AND STEELPAN

Ask a Trinbagonian what a xylopan means to the culture, and they probably won't be able to say exactly. However, the widely known steelpan is one of Trinidad's musical gifts to the world. It is recognized as the only acoustic instrument invented in the 20th century. The xylopan, created by Jomo Wahtuse circa 1983, is a steelpan innovation. It's a soprano pan surrounded by eight satellite pans.

The predecessor to the steelpan or xylopan is the tamboo bamboo (bamboo drum). In the 1880s, the colonial government outlawed drums used by both Afro and Indo Trinidadians. One of the many reasons why the regime tried to suppress their culture is because they also thought that African drums were secretly used to communicate messages.

The formerly enslaved invented the tamboo bamboo to counteract this. They used long hollowed-out bamboo tubes of varying sizes. Four sticks created different sounds: the boom (bass), foule (tenor), cutter (soprano), chandlers (alto). When played, they produced complex rhythmic arrangements. Tamboo bamboo bands were at the center of Kalinda and Carnival celebrations. Revelers often used a bottle and spoon to help keep rhythmic timing. This invention was the people's way to stay connected with their ancestors and resist colonial powers. By the 1930s, the tamboo bamboo bands were outlawed because of the violent clashes that erupted when rival bands met. People were still in search of artistic expression and experimented with recreating the sound with metal bins. This marked the beginning of the evolution of the steelband as we know it today.

While the xylopan is not widely known, Jomo won international acclaim for his jomoline steelpan invention. The Guinness Book of Records awarded him for creating the largest steelpan in the world. His steelpan, and contemporary iterations like the xylopan and jomoline are a beautiful representation of the resiliency of our people.

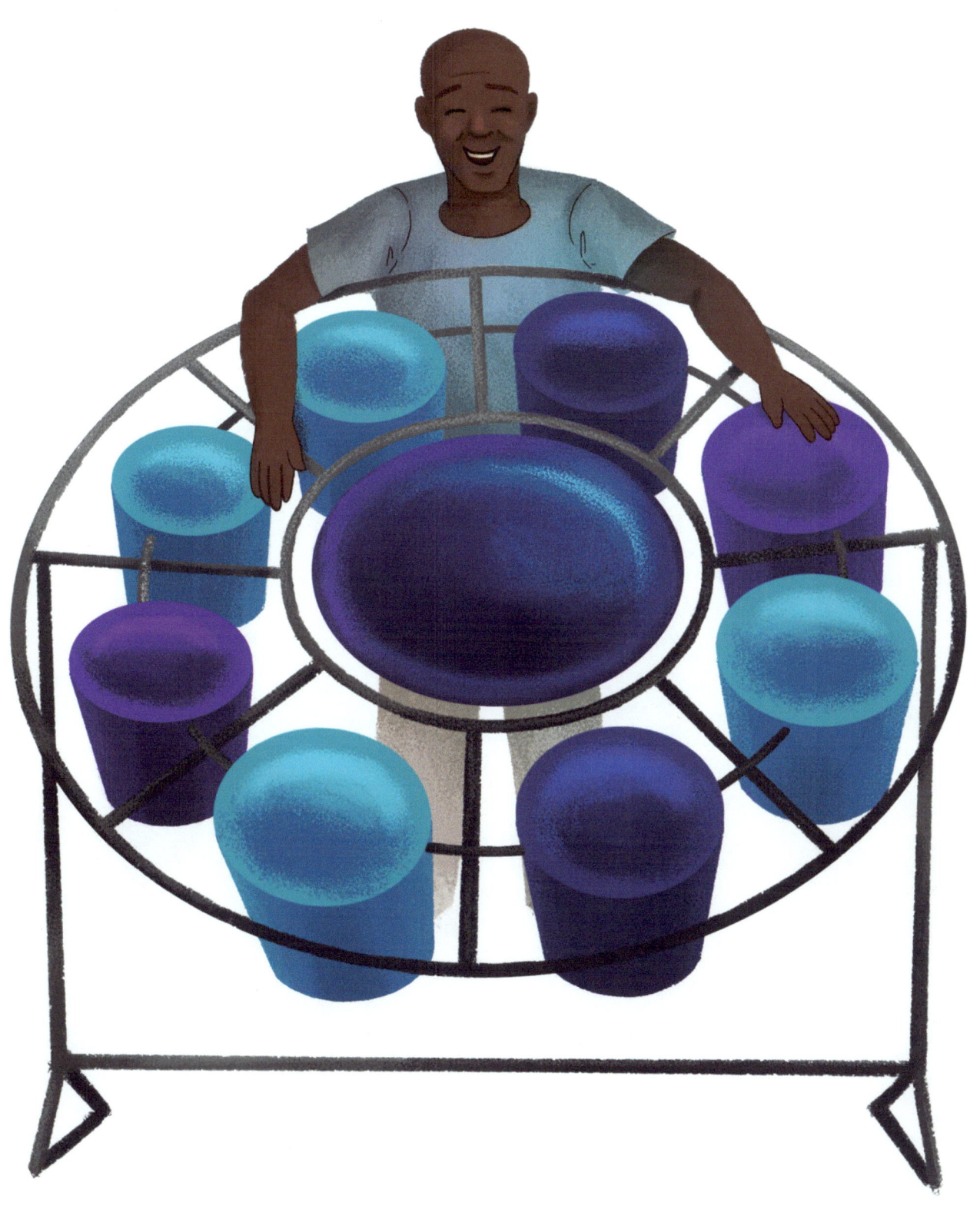

# YOUTH

The youth are the only way to memorialize and honor the culture. They are tomorrow's storytellers who can bridge the world of our past to our future. They are the ones who will preserve and celebrate our traditions. But they can only do this if we teach them the importance of heritage and pass on our ancestors' stories.

# ZESS

If you ask a Trini what 'zess' means, you'll get different responses depending on the age of the person you ask. In the late 1970s, calypsonian The Mighty Shadow was the self-proclaimed "zess man." Today there's an expanding definition of the word. Sometimes it's used to refer to local Trinidadian dancehall music or a party. Across the board, there's a consensus that zess is about raising positive vibes and high vibrations.

## ABOUT THE AUTHOR

Andrea Hall was born in Brooklyn, NY and migrated to Trinidad when she was a child. She spent her early childhood in Trinidad and later moved back to the U.S. Before writing *ABC's for the Little Trinis,* she's worked for digital publishers and fast-moving consumer goods companies connecting consumers to brands through impactful storytelling. She's passionate about curating and honoring Caribbean folklore and history for children and adults in Trinbago and across the diaspora. Stay up to date for additions and join the @abcsforthelittletrinis community on Instagram and Facebook.

www.ingramcontent.com/pod-product-compliance
Lightning Source LLC
Chambersburg PA
CBHW041537240626
47164CB00002B/38